Po...
Po...

Be...
Blackcurrant

Alice Apple

Peter
Potato

Grace Grape

Wee Willie
Water Melon

The Garden Gang
Stories and pictures by
Jayne Fisher

Other Garden Gang stories

Series 793

Avril Apricot

Ladybird Books Loughborough

Avril Apricot
had an awful problem.
Whenever
bedtime came,
no matter how hard
she tried,
she could not
fall asleep.
Poor Avril.
She would toss
and turn and sigh,
but whatever she did
only seemed
to make her
less and less sleepy.

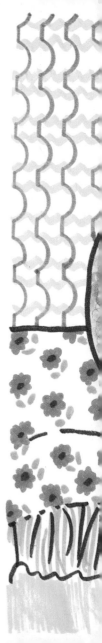

"I shall be
getting droopy eyes
and wrinkles
if I don't sleep soon,"
she said.
Betty Beetroot
was the first to notice
how tired
Avril was looking.
"Are you ill?" she asked.
"Oh no," said Avril,
trying to stifle
a huge yawn.
"I just can't manage
to sleep at night."

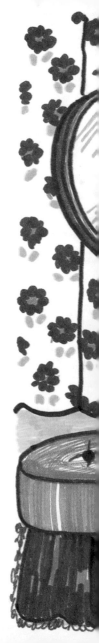

Betty, as you may
remember,
shares a house
with Polly Pomegranate
and as soon as
she got home
she told Polly
about Avril's problem.
Polly immediately said,
"She will have to sleep
in the daytime then.
She must have sleep."
But Avril had already
tried unsuccessfully
to sleep in the day.

Mark Marrow
was the next to hear
of Avril's problem.
"I imagine sheep
jumping over a stile
and count them,"
he said.
"It always works."
So that night,
Avril snuggled down
into her little bed,
closed her eyes
and started to count.
One, two, three . . .
four hundred and
sixty seven . . .
three thousand . . .

10

All through the night
Avril counted but
she could not sleep.
She dragged herself
out of bed
at six o'clock
and made herself
a nice cup of hot tea.
When Mark Marrow
met Avril
later that day,
he knew
by her tired face
that his idea
hadn't worked.

13

Mark worried about
poor Avril and told
some of his friends
about her.
They told their friends
and before long,
all the Garden Gang
knew about
Avril's problem.
They hurried to see her
with remedies
and ideas on how
she might get to sleep.
But nothing
seemed to work.

Lucy Leek suggested
that she did
a pile of washing
before going to bed.
Mrs Blackberry thought
that baking buns
was good for
making you sleep.
Bertie Brussels Sprout said
she ought to jog
around the garden.
Roger Radish
shyly suggested
swimming might help her.
Her mind was in a whirl
with all the advice.

She began to lose interest
in everything
because she was too tired
to think properly.
Her home began to
look neglected
and so did she.
Sometimes
she didn't even
bother to wash
and she hardly ever
went to the
Garden Gang meetings.
Everyone felt sorry
for her.

19

One evening,
at their weekly meeting,
the Garden Gang decided
to hold an orchestral
concert on the big lawn
behind the lily pond.
"The weather's warm,"
they said,
"and tomorrow afternoon
would be a good time
to hold it."
The members of the
Grace Grape Orchestra
were delighted
to be able to
perform again.

The next day, as the
orchestra members
made ready
for the concert,
a steady stream
of fruit and vegetables
made their way
onto the lawn
where they sat
in groups on the grass.
Penelope Strawberry
made sure that
Avril Apricot was there.
''The fresh air
will do you good,''
she said.

Bees droned
in and out of the flowers,
soft breezes blew,
sweet music filled the air
and guess
what happened . . .
Yes, Avril fell
fast asleep.
The Garden Gang
were so delighted
that as soon as
the concert ended,
they carried her home.
"Everything will be
fine now," they said,
as they tucked Avril
gently . . .

into her little bed!

Simon Swede

Simon Swede was sweet.
In fact he was so sweet
that everybody
loved him.
He always wore
trousers which were
much too short.
Although he had
grown out of them
he said they were
very comfortable
and that it was
more important
to feel comfortable
than to look smart.

Simon was fond
of all living creatures
and was always kind
and gentle to them.
Once, he made friends
with a grasshopper,
but after a few days
the lively creature
hopped off into the
long undergrowth
and was gone.
Simon was sad
and looked for
another pet.

He only had to
speak to a cat
and it would
follow him home.
His parents
often found it
embarrassing
when they had to   ,
return a struggling cat
to the place where Simon
had first seen it,
hoping that it would
return to its
rightful owner.

One day a hedgehog
wandered
across the garden
and before you could say,
"Prickly Pete", Simon
was there chatting.
"Will you be my pet?"
he said.
"Sorry," said
the hedgehog,
"but I'm afraid
I shall be too busy.
Come along children."
Out of the flower bed
wobbled five fat babies.

Simon Swede's
chief love was dogs.
He thought and
talked about them
all day
and dreamed
about them all night.
Simon was a very
athletic little Swede
and pictured himself
running through the
cool, shady woods
with his dog
by his side.
Oh, what fun
they could have.

"Please, oh please
may I have a dog?"
he asked
his Mum and Dad
one morning at breakfast.
"No," they told him,
"we don't think
you are old enough yet."
"But I am," said Simon,
"and I promise
I would take
very good care
of him."
But still
they said, "No."

It was Autumn time
and the red
and yellow leaves
were fluttering
from the trees
and forming
a colourful carpet
on the flower beds and
lawns of the garden.
Simon was leaping
and jumping across
the orchard, in his
usual energetic way
when, from behind
a tree, came a
whimpering sound.

41

Simon peeped
round the tree and was
surprised to see
Spot, the dog,
who belonged to
Mr Rake the gardener.
His leg was caught
beneath the tree roots
and he was covered
in wet, sticky mud.
Simon soon had
Spot's leg free.
"You can't go home
like that," he said.
"Come with me."

Spot obediently
went to Simon's house
and there Simon bathed,
dried and brushed him
until he looked smarter
than he had
ever looked before.
"You can
go home now, Spot,"
said Simon,
and off Spot went.
Mr and Mrs Swede
were so proud
of their little son.
"He's so sensible,"
they said.

The Garden Gang
were becoming more
and more excited
each day
because it would
soon be Christmas.
Mums were making
Christmas cakes,
plum puddings
and mince pies,
and the children
were helping by being
especially good.
Dads were sawing
logs for the fireside
and some were
making toys.

47

Simon Swede
looked out of his
bedroom window
on Christmas Eve.
The garden was
bathed in moonlight
and everything
was peaceful.
He still felt
a twinge of sadness
at not having a pet.
''Never mind,
it's Christmas Day
tomorrow,'' he thought,
''and I'm sure to get
a lovely present.''
He did! . . .

49

Waiting for him was a

cuddly puppy dog!

Paul Pumpkin

Bertie Brussels Sprout

Mark Marrow

Gertru
Goosebe

Tim Tomato

Patrick Pear

Avril Apricot